DADDY'S PUNISHMENT

ERORICA FOR WOMEN SHORT,DADDY BREEDS HIS LITTLE GIRL

BY

STONY RIDERS

TABLE OF CONTENTS

CHAPTER 1

Frank had finally had enough of his step daughter and her pranks since he got married to Rita a year ago.

“Doesn’t it get old?”Frank asked giving her the bra he found in his wardrobe

“Pervert,how’d you get that?” Stella asked

“I know you put in my wardrobe Ella” he said throwing it to her

“I’m here to stay little pest, stop with all this petty stunts you’re pulling” he said heading back to his room

“Here to stay uhn? Let’s see about that” she said.

“Rita, your hubby is stealing my bra!!!” She yelled to Rita who was making dinner downstairs

“Ooooh please Ella what does frank what with your bras! “ Rita asked already getting tired of their little fights

“I dunno ask him!” She snorted back as she began going down the stairs

“Your husband is a pervert” she said rudely

“Enough with your games Stella I am genuinely tired of it” Frank said irritated

“Ok Ella, Frank is no longer pleased with your games. I think it’s time to grow up,you know? Because you are 19 years old. No longer a child” Rita said sarcastically to her daughter who was on the end of the dining table pouting her lips in defeat.

She never really won this game she started since Frank and Rita started to date,but she wasn’t one to give up that easily.

She knew that one day she’d be successful and get what she wanted from Rita,which was an intense argument which would make them break off their relationship.

CHAPTER 2

Three months later.

"How dare you?!" Rita shouted at frank.

"Babe it's not what it looks like!" Frank said, rushing down the staircase as he tried to catch up with Rita who was running away.

Stella just stood there smiling knowing she had achieved what she had always wanted and it felt good to know Rita would never forgive Frank.

Little did she know that this offense would come with a suitable punishment.

Back to the present.

They had all gathered at the table to eat dinner after Rita was done cooking and everyone ate silently while Rita observed her baby girl was quiet.

She just knew she must be plotting something new against her husband so she knew she'd have to tell her something to change her mind.

"Ella dear?" She said sweetly

"Hmmm?" Stella replied coldly.

"That's no way to respond to your mother" Frank said strictly

"Leave the fatherly duties to my father thank you " Stella snapped back

"Okay enough! You two " Rita said disappointed that it's been a year and Stella hadn't still bonded with her step father unless you consider constant sketching of bad things bonding.

"Ella,I am happy here. I am good with Frank ,even if you don't like him,you should at least like him for me because he makes me happy" she said calmly

"Hmmm... was that before or after you cheated on dad with him?" She asked coldly

“My marriage with your dad was already ending at the point I met Frank baby” Rita said

“Maybe he’s the reason why it ended-“ Stella was saying before Rita lost her temper and interrupted Stella

“Enough Ella you can blame me all you want but don’t blame this marriage “ Rita said pained

“News flash momma,a marriage built on cheating is doomed to end in cheating. I don’t like Frank you do. Don’t expect me to like him just because you like him”Stella said

“I don’t want you to like him, I want you to respect me and my marriage” she snapped back

“Ok mum.” She said as she left the dining table with her food barely touched and made way for her room.

Frank and Rita stared at each other for sometime and she mouthed the words “I’m sorry “ to him which he smiled at and went back to eating his food.

He knew he had to do something to make Stella come over to his side but he really didn't know what else to do,he had begged her and threatened her in the past already he had no idea how to get through to her that he loves her mum.

He knew she wasn't stopping there anytime soon so he was already prepared for what else he was going to see in his room.

Days and weeks passed and nobody heard a bit of a noise in the Tareda house.

Rita was surprised about the improvements,no more immature stunts,no arguing,no curse words. Nothing at all from Stella's end and she was beginning to think she actually got to her daughter after the last conversation.

It was even better considering the fact that she was now respectful to Frank.

But Rita might have bought it but Frank knew she was just waiting for when to strike.

He began to get shocked at her progress,it's been 2 months since he'd been on his guard. Maybe she had grown.

She came to have a conversation about her boyfriend in school,Pete and he began to think that perhaps her relationship with Pete was the reason why she was now less interested in him and his wife's relationship. Finally she had grown and was now mature.

She'd tell her mum of how Frank advised her about Pete, her new boyfriend and make her mother see that she and Frank were now as tight as ever before.

But little did they both know she was just plotting and knew she needed their trust to be able to achieve this feat because it was a very big plan.

It was more than panties in his bag or his underwear in her room,she was going big or going home this time around and she had a very good feeling she was going to come out the winner after the challenge against

Frank,and Pete was not existing by the way. I thought you should know.

CHAPTER 3

Some days later,seeing that they both now trusted her fully she decided to put her plan in motion.

“Mum?” She called for Rita

“Yes baby girl”

“I have something I want to tell you” Stella said.

Rita listened on seeing her daughter was all too calm and seeming scared.

As Stella was about to tell her what she had in mind she started to fake her tears. Acting like it was too much for her to say.

Rita consoled her and urged her to tell her what’s wrong.

“I’m scared if I tell you this you’ll hate me” she said still crying

“Hate you? I can never hate my daughter. You know that “ Rita said, bothered about Stella.

“Mum…. Frank touched me yesterday “ she said calmly

Rita was caught in shock and disbelief

“But he’d never do something like that “ she muttered confused.

A part of Rita believed because of the state she saw her daughter in and the fact that Stella had been really close to her step dad for a while.

She saw Rita burst out to tears and continued to console her.

“I know you’d not believe me,I know you hate me now” Stella faked.

“No baby, it's just so much to take in,that’s all. I believe you” Rita said amidst confusion

“Tomorrow,I’ll be home sick. Come back in two hours and you can see for yourself that your husband molested me”Stella said sniffing and closing her fake act.

This time around she wasn’t gonna lose it's time for her to play just enough to make her mother jealous enough to want to be single again. Frank's time was becoming sickening for her and her daddy had already told her that Frank was the reason he and her mum couldn't get back together again and she wanted her father back. Not some hot stranger acting like he owned the place.

The next day Stella decided to sleep in,Frank had to check up on her and found out her body was hurting her, he cared for her for a bit before heading down the stairs.

"Ella is sick babe,I think I should stay home to see how she's fending " Frank said.

"You sure that's why you want to stay home?" Rita asked

Her question took Frank by surprise.

"Is something wrong between us?" He asked, feeling disturbed.

There was an erring silence in the kitchen. As soon as Rita was done with breakfast she moved up to shower.

She had only thoughts of what happened between her daughter and her yesterday in her head. She kept relieving how frightened she was,and she began to wonder if it was true.

If her husband was molesting his step daughter,a part of her didn't want to believe it but a part of her didn't want to see her daughter sexually molested.

She got dressed and left the house without saying a word to Frank.

She only went into Ella's room to check for her and to tell her she loved her. And after that she left for work.

Frank had been confused about everything and still was confused but he felt she'd come and talk things through with him when she was ready.

He got Stella's food from the kitchen and took it to her room.

Stella had already set an alarm for 1 hour and 50 minutes since her mother left.

He brought her food 30 minutes after Rita left so she ate it and rested back into her bed.

An hour had passed and 20 minutes were left so she removed her clothes and was naked. Went to lock her room door partially enough to be broken with force and waited till the alarm rang and she screamed.

“What the hell is this?!” She yelled as loud as she could

Frank was shocked and rushed to her room.

“There is something in my body Frank!!!!” She yelled as she cried.

“What is the wrong?!” Frank shouted from behind the door as he saw it was locked.

“I don’t know what's wrong Frank but it hurts!” She shouted as she cried out her eyes.

Frank out of fear broke down the door and came to see Stella,he was first taken aback by the fact that she had no clothing on but as he saw her irritated in her own skin the thought of helping her made him come closer.

“What is wrong?” He asked concerned seeing how she was crying

“Something hurts in here” she said, pointing at her boobs.

He stood there hesitant of what a minute he felt like he had to do but then seeing her cry he felt like he needed to feel what she said felt like a stone in her breast.

Rita on the other hand was already back and moving up the stairs speedily because of the sounds she heard from upstairs which seemed like her daughter crying.

“Your breast seems fine to me” Frank said, unable to resist the hard on he felt forming up from feeling the boobs of his step daughter and realizing that the girl was actually very hot.

“Feel it here it hurts there “ she said moving her hands on his forcefully making him touch her breast while she waited on Rita.

She was hoping she'd walk in on them anytime soon.

When she saw Rita standing in front of the room, shocked at what she seemed to be looking at, she pushed his hands away and screamed and cried.

"Leave me alone you pervert!" She said as she fell to the floor in tears and agony

Frank, who at some point was enjoying the feel of her boobs, woke up from the statement "pervert" and was wondering what was wrong. It was until he heard Rita yell he knew this was all a plot to begin with.

CHAPTER 4

“How dare you!!” She yelled with tears in her eyes,pain in her voice and anger all over her face.

He turned to Stella who was now standing with a smile on her face and rushed to pursue his wife.

“Babe, it's not what it looks like!” He said rushing down the stairs to catch up with her.

“I can’t believe I trusted you over my own daughter!” Rita cried, hurt and heartbroken.

She rushed into her car and drove off.

Frank angrily walked back up to see Stella dressing up like nothing ever happened.

“This was all your ruse to get me out of your mum’s life?” He asked disappointed at her cold hearted features.

"I'm pretty sure it worked" she said putting on her shirt

"Since you said I'm a pervert,a rape. Lemme help you make it true." He said, tearing off her shirt.

"What the hell is wrong with you Frank?!" She yelled.

He slapped her and instructed her to keep shut "I'm a pervert right,let me do what pervert does " he continued as he pulled off his pants and forcefully removed hers.

She had no idea that the stunt she played made him horny as she would never have thought he was attracted to her,and to be honest neither would he.

But getting to feel her boobs totally changed his perspective and the fact that he was sure his marriage was over made him see that he stands the chance to lose nothing if he made love to his step daughter.

He was lustful and angry and she was both the cause and the victim.

He held her head down and forced her to get on her knees.

“Please stop it, frankly,I’ll tell her I lied” she said crying at how her plan worked too well.

“What will that change?” He asked as he forced her mouth into his hard and throbbing dick and began to moving her head in and out of his dick, he started slowly at first and then soon he began to move faster not caring if she’d choke down there,when she forced her mouth out of his dick to catch her breathe,he forced it back inside.

“Choke on my dick like you should’ve choked on your constant lies” he said in a mix of anger and pleasure.

“Spit on it” he instructed as he removed her mouth from his dick letting her catch her breath.

She started to use her hands to stroke his dick and she seemed exemplarily skilled on that particular aspect.

She gripped his dick tightly and moved front and back with both her palm while her mouth was on his balls. She began to stroke harder and harder until he began to feel the cum build up in his dick.

He took his dick from her and started stroking it himself and made sure he came on her face.

“This here is your punishment “ he said as he filled her face with his cum.

“I’m here to stay Stella,I’m still gonna be your daddy”he said as he picked her up from the floor and placed her in a doggy position.

“And you know what you will do for me?” He asked as he forced his dick into her surprisingly tight pussy and he heard a loud cry from her as he himself let out a satisfying moan.

“You’ll tell mummy that it was all a lie and that you faked everything “ he said as he started to stroke her incredibly wet and tight pussy.

“But you are fucking me Frank! “ she said crying out

“Am I?” He asked as he wiped her ass hardly and she screamed in pain

“No!!” She cried.

He began moving his dick in and out of her pussy,unable to help the pleasure he was feeling from the tightness of her pussy.

While she didn’t seem to be having a pleasant time,but punishment shouldn’t be enjoyed in the first place and this was his punishment for being a bad girl, it was her *DADDY’S PUNISHMENT* but he’d be faking it if he said he wasn’t having the time of his life with his step daughter right now.

He quickly laid face up and asked her to ride him,he didn’t want to see her crying face so he put her in the reverse cowgirl position.

Anytime she slowed down from the pain he made sure to wipe her ass hard and ensured she moved at the speed he loved.

“Haven’t you done this with Pete before, why are you crying ?” He asked as he enjoyed every bit of how new her pussy felt

"Who's Pete?" She asked as the pain started to reduce a little on her end and she began to feel the sweetness of his dick in her pussy.

"Your boyfriend " he moaned out as he noticed her speed was now increasing and the sex was becoming more and more pleasing.

"I'm going to cum" he said as her speed was making him attain orgasm.

"Please don't cum" Stella begged as she was just starting to enjoy the sex.

She stopped riding him immediately and allowed the excitement to die down a bit before she turned to a cowgirl pose to start kissing him.

"I never realized I could enjoy my punishment so much" she whispered in his ear as she started to kiss him.

"Make love to me Frank and I'll tell Rita that I planned everything." She said after kissing him intimately.

He wondered where this was coming from since she was crying initially.

“Is this your first time?” He asked her, realizing that,it must be the reason as to why she didn’t enjoy the feeling of him inside her initially.

She nodded her head shyly to the question. Then let me make it your best he said as he immediately lifted her off his body and placed her face up on her bed.

He started to make love to her body gently and slowly and made sure he made most of the first and probably not last sex he was having with his step daughter.

She moaned at all the feel of the body he touched with his lips,she made sure she enjoyed every bit of his relieving touch.

“I love this” she moaned in excitement

“I know you would” he whispered in her ear.

As he made to kiss her intimately,holding his breath as his face stayed tight to hers till they felt like they couldn’t breathe anymore from the deepness of the kiss.

He used his tongue to seductively trace from her face to her pussy,and he began to suck on her clits gently but passionately.

She let out a loud moan as he fed on her forbidden food.

He brought out his middle finger and began to move in and out of her pussy slowly at first so she’d not endure any further pain and started moving faster as he continued further.

Her screams began to feel the room.

“ I want you” she said as she couldn’t wait anymore to feel that dick inside her again.

He brought his dick and began to rub it against her clit in a bid to lubricate it with the wetness of her pussy.

She moaned from the touch of his hard dick against her pussy.

When his dick entered inside her pussy she let out a loud moan to show how much more she was enjoying Frank's dick inside her,her moan got louder and louder.

"Let's never stop this!" She yelled.

That moan was what Rita heard as she stepped back into the house after having cried out her eyes because of what she saw before.

"We won't have to stop this baby girl, because you'll tell Rita that it's a lie right? " Frank said in utmost pleasure.

"It's you I love now Stella, I'll make sure Rita doesn't end things so we can be together. You want that too right?" He said to Stella

"Yes daddy I do" she moaned as they both had themselves in a missionary position.

Rita on the other hand stood beside the wall listening to all the moans of pleasure they made and the part of her that believed Frank died instantly.

Frank turned Stella to the side and started to fuck her from the side as she was overwhelmed by the skills the old man could do with the big dick of his.

“Now I know why mummy won’t let you go,you fuck me like you own me Frank “ she said while Rita watched as tears dropped down her eyes

“Your pussy tastes better than your mum’s” he said as he could feel the cum build up in his dick.

“I’m gonna cum daddy!!” She screamed

“Just keep fucking me like that daddy” she screamed.

“Ooooh really!!” Rita yelled

“Wait mummy I’m gonna cum” Stella kept shouting

“I’m gonna fucking cum inside you baby” Frank moaned they both didn’t care that Rita was watching them.

“Ooooh fuck!” They yelled

And fell back to the bed.

“Are you done?” Rita said as they turned back in shock.

“You came right? Now it’s time to go Frank,get out of my house! “ Rita yelled

“Mum, it's not what it looks like” Stella said, putting on her clothes.

“It’s fake rii,you made it all up rii? Ya I know already” Stella said

“You and I are getting a divorce Frank “ Stella said

“You are not going to be the one that will mess up my daughter” Stella continued

“Ella you’ve had your fun,we’re getting back together with daddy” she said as she left the room

“Mum please no!!! Frank is a good man,this was all me. And I won’t do it again” she cried

“Y’a I know, good in bed.” Rita said

"I'm sorry I didn't listen to you before baby girl,now he has messed you up" Rita continued.

"No mum I want it" Stella said

"Shut up!!! This minute" Rita yelled

"I'm grown up enough to know what I want mummy" Stella said as she went to Frank to kiss him right in front of Rita.

It was now Rita saw that this was the beginning of something truly ugly.

Made in the USA
Monee, IL
06 May 2025

16942077R00017